My first monster book has sold so well,
I bought a gold guitar.
Then I had some people fit
a second story on my car.
And now my mansion has a track
where men on Jet Skis race giraffes.
(I also held some money back
to throw at pigeons, just for laughs.)

So, when asked if Frank could write some more,
I told myself, I quote,
> If that freak will
> make a sequel,
> I can buy a bigger boat!

(He's the poet—did you know it?
You deserve an explanation:
Frankenstein does all the writing.
I provide the motivation.)

So, I said to him, "More poems!"
But he raised his hand (which shook,
due to a writer's cramp he'd picked up
working on the Sandwich book),
and said, "*No* poems. Poems bad.
I think I ready to retire.
Maybe travel. Start a hobby."
To which I responded, *"FIRE!"*

Then I waved around a burning torch—
that always does the trick.
Frankenstein got right to writing rhymes,
and wrote them all right quick.

So, as long as they keep sending checks,
I am
> Yours truly,

A Message from

Adam Rex

Program

The Mother-in-Law of **FRANKENSTEIN** Makes Wedding Plans

WE'VE A LOT OF CATCHING UP TO DO. I HOPE MY FOLKS ARE THERE.
I CAN'T WAIT TO SEE THEIR FACES. THEY DON'T KNOW I CHANGED MY HAIR.
After all I've done arranging for your funeral and flowers,
and you're only dead for—what?
An afternoon? A couple hours?
MOTHER,
LIGHTNING MADE ME LIVE AGAIN, AND NOW I'M GETTING MARRIED!
Do you know how much it cost to get you boxed, embalmed, and buried?
Well, a lot—
enough to put me and your father deep in debt—
and now we have to plan your wedding? To a man I've never met?

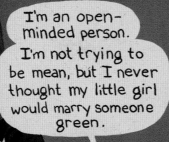

OFF THE TOP OF MY HEAD

THE OFFICIAL BLOG OF THE HEADLESS HORSEMAN

10/05/08

Please Stop Staring at My Delicious Head

It's sup*posed* to be scary, you know.

Headless Horseman
VIEW MY PROFILE

LINKS

I Vant to Suck Your Blog

Monsters.com

The Blog Lagoon

Hagslist

Frankenblog

The Hunchblog of Notre Dame

Slasherdot

But this morning I rode by a little café, and it said pumpkin bisque was their soup of the day. As I passed, the chef stared in the creepiest way.

Heaven knows how the crows always find me.
Or the pigeons that fly by but sneak up behind me,
then poke in their heads
to pick seeds through my eyes.
And although I hate pigeons,
I *really* despise
how the crows go all Hitchcock,
and day turns to night
as they claw and they caw
and they snap and they bite
and then back to the branches
or god knows what place;
and the flapping's like clapping,
the caws are applause
for my big, orange, delectable face.

And these grandmas
won't leave me alone.
They surround me and talk
about muffins and bread.
Or they hound me with
piecrusts and poke at my head.
"It's a good one," they whisper.
I wish I was dead.

THE SPHINX
AIN'T ALL THAT—
YEAH, YOU HEARD ME

I'm just saying, the Sphinx
ain't as great as she thinks.

Her Egyptian hat thing
is all covered in bling,
and she has a nice face,
but I'll cut to the chase:

From her neck to her *butt*,
she don't look like King Tut.

And
because
of the Sphinx,
all of Egypt now stinks.
You can follow your nose
to the places she goes:
in the Nile, on a pyramid, *anywhere* here amid
all of the sand of her litter-box land.

While you're cleaning her mess, she'll invite you to guess:

What has four legs at dawn
only two later on,
*and then three legs at night?**

She'll just yawn if you're right;
if you're *not* good at riddles,
then you're
Tender
Vittles.

AN EDGAR ALLAN POEM

At midnight, Poe's reciting parts of poetry he's writing,
whilst a raven is alighting on the bust above his door.
But the poem Poe composes poses problems, 'cause he knows his
line on roses being roses has been written once before.
He sup*poses* he could change it—he had lots of rhymes before.
Tons of choices. Rhymes galore.

In his bleary brain he goes through all the words that rhyme with *rose*,
and throws out *clothes, expose, Joe's, nose,* and *toes,* and maybe twenty more.
Alas, in spite of all of those, he sees not one of them that flows
as well as *rose is rose is rose,* the line he used to have before.
"Maybe I should switch to prose," he sighs, and lies down on the floor.
Quoth the raven,

"What a bore."

MELTING the inches away...

"I'm melting...

Before

After

and with only one bucket of water a day!"

DIET? Don't try it!
You've heard all the pitches.
They promise results,
but they don't work for witches.
Well, now there's a way
to stay bony and gaunt
and still eat all the houses
and children you want!
So, call your hag sister
and tell your witch daughter—

they're going to get sickly
more quickly with WATER!
Here's how it works:
Send our coupon by mail,
and in four to six weeks
we'll deliver your pail.
Fill the pail up with water
and *tighten your belt*
as you soak yourself silly
and watch the pounds melt!

✓ YES! ▭ ◕ ☎

I would like to be thin as a rail.
Please send me your patented bucket by mail.

Consult your witch doctor if skin begins smoking,
or melting persists for three hours after soaking.
In rare cases witches melt down to their toes so that
nothing is left but their shoes, hat, and clothes.

NEW GLASSES

In her classes, without glasses,
she could barely see the board.
With her specs she checks the teachers,
sees their frightened, frozen features—

Oh. So *that's* why,
when she raised her hand,
Medusa was ignored.

10/23/08

Real Original, Jerks

I was first to go headless.

I started the trend.

I remember a time

when a person could shout,

"Hey! That guy has no head!

It's a pumpkin instead!"

and you'd know it was me

he was talking about.

But this morning I'm riding

my horse into work

and this Headless Accountant

is walking his dog.

And although it's still dark,

I can see, in the park,

that the Headless Vice-Principal's

out for a jog.

HORSEMAN HEADLESS

Local horseman has no head – *but he has a big heart.*

SLEEPY HOLLOW - People may stop and stare, point...even run away in fear. But that hasn't stopped one local man from pursuing his dream of decapitating

Headless Horseman
VIEW MY PROFILE

LINKS

I Vant to Suck Your Blog

Monsters.com

The Blog Lagoon

Hagslist

Frankenblog

The Hunchblog of
Notre Dame

Slasherdot

There's a woman in town
who's a Headless Headmistress.
She's dating the mayor
(a bodiless head).
And I bet you a dollar
they're joined at the collar
this June,
when the two of them wed.

You must tell me *where*
you all get your ideas.
This whole no-head thing
is just really fantastic.
And pumpkins with faces!
On *necks* of all places!
(In case you can't tell it,
I'm being sarcastic.)

EDGAR ALLAN POE
SHOULD BE WRITING OR SLEEPING,
NOT DOING A CROSSWORD PUZZLE

Oh, Poe *knows* he should be working on the poet work he's shirking,
whilst the raven still is lurking on the bust above his door.
It's just 7-Down that keeps our peep from getting any sleep:
"'Crusading wife of former veep?' I'm sure I've had this one before!
But what the devil is a *veep?*" he weeps, as lo, the clock strikes four.
Quoth the raven,

"Tipper Gore."

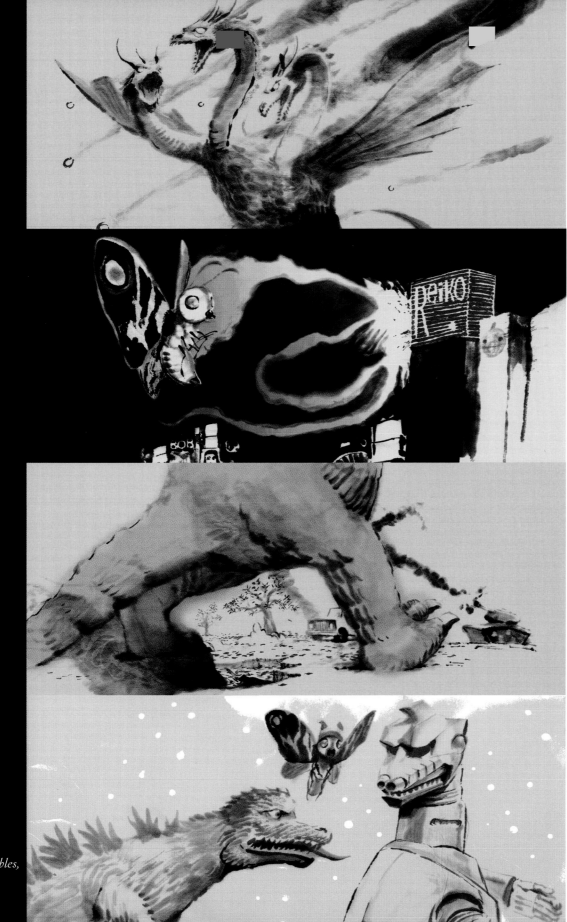

KAIJU HAIKU*

Forget the flowers—
April *meteor* showers
bring gold space dragons.

Tokyo summer.
Mothra flies into a sign
again and again.

An autumn rampage,
the sound of leaves and soldiers
crunching underfoot.

A winter wager:
Will Godzilla's tongue freeze to
Mechagodzilla?

19

E.T.-MAIL

We assumed it was the case
that in a place as big as space
we'd find some trace of other races
with our scientific bases.

When a signal was detected,
it was not what we expected.
In the subject line it pleaded,
PLEASE REPLY—
          ASSISTANCE NEEDED

SALUTATIONS TO YOUR HEALTH.
PLEASE HELP ME TRANSFER ALL MY WEALTH
INTO YOUR BANK ACCOUNT ON EARTH—
ELEVEN MILLION DOLLARS' WORTH.
I NEED YOUR ANSWER RIGHT AWAY.
PLEASE SEND A LETTER BACK TODAY
(ALONG WITH FIFTY DOLLARS, PLEASE,
TO PAY THE MONEY-TRANSFER FEES).

We gasped—a message from the stars!
And then another came from Mars:
NEED BIGGER, YELLOWER ANTENNAE?
HAVE TOO FEW OR HAVE TOO MANY?
LOSS OF VIGOR? LOUSY SLEEPER?
OUR PRESCRIPTION DRUGS ARE *CHEAPER*!!!

We were noticing a pattern,
when a bunch arrived from Saturn:
FANCY WATCHES! CLICK AND SEE!
and GET YOUR HYPERSCHOOL DEGREE.

At *SINGLES IN YOUR SECTOR!!!*
we disabled our detector.
Then we emptied out the cache
and dragged the letters to the trash.

So, that's the fact we had to face:
There's no intelligence in space.
But that's okay—for what it's worth,
there isn't much of it on Earth.

OFF THE TOP OF MY HEAD

THE OFFICIAL BLOG OF THE HEADLESS HORSEMAN

11/01/08

Maybe It's Time I Changed This Pumpkin

It's been sagging,
slowly browning,
and it looks
just like I'm frowning.
On the stem I've pinned
some paper pines—
they help the stink,
I think.

But these trees
can't hide the funk in-
side this sad and
sunken punkin,

Headless Horseman
VIEW MY PROFILE

LINKS

I Vant to Suck Your Blog

Monsters.com

The Blog Lagoon

Hagslist

Frankenblog

The Hunchblog of
Notre Dame

Slasherdot

But! Too late
do I remember
it's the first day
of November,
and the stock boy
at the store
says, "There's no
pumpkins anymore."
So, now he delves
into the shelves
to see what sort
of fruit might suit.

Alas, I hate the color of the lime.
The orange is orange but doesn't rhyme.
The kiwi is too peewee — there's no space to carve a face.

And it seems that I've forgotten:
Every fruit, in time, goes rotten.
Every gourd, ignored, will —
Wait, what's this?
What has the stock boy gotten?

No One Comes to SKULL ISLAND Anymore

We're easy to find—you just sail for a day
through this reef full of interesting,
razor-sharp rocks.
I don't know **why** the tourists are staying away.
There's not **one single ship** at the docks.
Tell your friends! We have acres of beautiful beaches.
And more pterodactyls than ever before!
Plus enormous mosquitoes and blood-sucking leeches!
Do people not like giant bugs anymore?
No, that's **silly**. There has to be some other reason.
The insects are great—all the dinosaurs, too.
But regardless, it's still been a really slow season.
The poor things have nothing to do.

Once a week there's a luau,
and some girl or guy
will get strung way up high where they're easy to see.
Then they're offered to whichever monster stops by.
If you're chosen, your dinner is free!

And **oh**, what a dinner!
Hot bat wings and bread!
Pupu platter and mangoes!
Roast beetle and pork!
I just can't understand
why the island's so dead—

even Kong went
and moved to
New York.

20c

No ghosts are seen on Halloween,
except for kids in sheets.
No zombies ring for anything
apart from tricks or treats.
Though people say
today's the day
when bogeymen
come out to play,

November first is when the worst
of monsters hit the streets.

And in disguise the dead arise
to sell us magazines.
In ties and slacks
they hand out tracts
as fine, upstanding teens.
Just like the kids the night before,
these horrors go from door to door
with vacuums, mops, or other props,
and boring sales routines.

It might feel mean on Folloween
to just ignore your door.
"A Girl Scout troop is on my stoop,"
you'll mutter,
"nothing more."
You want a snack so bad it hurts,
but trust me—
those are ghouls in skirts.
With that in mind
you'll find
you're not so
hungry anymore.

The Frankenstein Wedding Suite

The Caterer of Frankenstein
Makes an Announcement

The Flower Girl of Frankenstein
Makes a Scene

The Bride of Frankenstein
Wrote Her Own Vows

The Best Man of Frankenstein
Makes a Trip to the Buffet

THE CATERER OF FRANKENSTEIN MAKES AN ANNOUNCEMENT

Listen *up*! This is the day we've been dreading:
We're serving the guests of the Frankenstein wedding.
So, please heed these warnings and plan for the worst,
if you want to avoid getting eaten or cursed.

The Black Lagoon creature has no self-control,
so be careful you don't drop too much in his bowl,
or he'll eat and he'll eat and he'll eat and won't stop
till he bloats and then floats belly-up on the top.

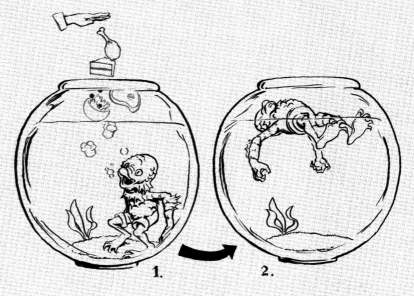

Don't say "steak" to the vampires—they won't understand.
They'll just look for a sharp piece of wood in your hand.
And don't give them garlic—we seem to be missing
a list of their symptoms
(apart from the hissing
and bat transformations
and all of the hassle
of chasing them half the way
back to their castle).

The wolfmen hate silverware. Don't give it to them.
No drinks for the skeletons—wine goes right through them.

Let's see now. . . is that all I wanted to say?
Oh! We're no longer serving the cherries flambé.
Yes, I know this is coming right down to the wire,
but the Frankenstein family has problems with fire.

1.   2.

The Flower Girl of Frankenstein Makes a Scene

The Bride of Frankenstein
Wrote Her Own Vows

Already? The vows? I don't know where to start.
In the old days, when I was still young (and alive),
I would dream of my wedding. I planned every part.
When I died, I was sure it would never arrive.
Now I'm back, and expected to give up my heart
to a flat-headed giant as green as a chive.

Which is fair, I suppose, since he gave me his, first.
In a box. Just the thought of it's making me queasy.
It feels like my *own* heart is ready to burst,
and yet somehow I don't think I'll get off that easy.
I'm sorry. It's not going like I rehearsed,
but that garbage I wrote about love was so cheesy.

Okay, so you're probably wondering why
I'm still standing up here, after all that I've said.
When we met, I'll admit, I came off a bit...shy.
But he fondled my hand and sighed,
     "YOU GOOD. US WED?"
And he's sweet and he's tall, so I'll marry the guy.
'Cause let's face it—I'm not getting any less dead.

THE BEST MAN
OF FRANKENSTEIN
MAKES A TRIP
TO THE BUFFET

Let us see vhat we have…carrot soup (very nice)
London broil, chocolate fountain, some kind of a rice,
cheese and fruit—ah, that's cute: little coffin-shaped cakes.
The chilled rum of the night—vhat sweet punch it makes!

Hey, vhat's this? It's like toast. I vill try a small bite.
Most unusual. Pungent. Yet something's not right.
Madam, vhat's on this bread?
Yes, yes, butter…uh-huh.
Also garlic, and—wait.
This is *GARLIC* BREAD?!

BLUH!

I have allergies, dolt! And I thought we vere clear—
I vas told it was safe to try everything here!
Vhat became of the list that I gave to your bosses?
I'm not to have garlic, wheat, peanuts, or crosses!

I vill *not* "calm down." I vill go right on yelling—
Ooooh boy…here we go. First the hives, then the svelling.
Ooooh, vhere's my inhaler? It's not in my vest.
Vas it there vhen I dressed? Vhen I had my vest pressed?

Vhen I had my tuxedo repaired at the tailor?
HELLO! Um, has anyvone theen muh inhaluh?

EDGAR ALLAN POE
HEARS SWEET MUSIC
LIKE THE DULCET TONES
OF ANGELS OR WHATEVER

"Hark!" said Poe. "I hear a dinging, as if wedding bells were ringing, and the heartsick thoughts they're bringing sting of love I lost before. And there! Again there comes a bell, as if the heavens long to tell about the pale and radiant belle that bards and beggars called Lenore; and again it rings and sings of dead, drowned, lovely, lost Lenore." Quoth the raven,

"GET THE *DOOR!*"

Ya stupid poet.

Library of Congress Cataloging-in-Publication Data
Rex, Adam.
Frankenstein takes the cake/by Adam Rex.
p.   cm.
1. Monsters—Juvenile poetry.
2. Children's poetry, American.   I. Title.
PS3618.E925F75   2008
811′.6—dc22   2007044634
ISBN 978-0-15-206235-4

First edition
H G F E D C B A

The illustrations in this book were done in pencil,
charcoal, oils, and, in many cases, in Photoshop with
a Wacom tablet. And probably some other things.
The display lettering was created by Adam Rex.
The text type was set in PastonchiMT.
Color separations by Colourscan Co. Pte. Ltd., Singapore
Manufactured by South China Printing Company, Ltd., China
Production supervision by Pascha Gerlinger
Designed by April Ward and Jennifer Kelly

For the Bride of the Author

POEMS THAT DO NOT
APPEAR IN THIS VOLUME

The Fifty-Foot Woman Wants to Know If
This Circus Tent Makes Her Look Fat

Smeleton

King Kong Would Like to Have Just One Date That
Doesn't End with Him Getting Shot at by Airplanes

Bigfoot and the Yeti Can't Believe
You Sat Them at the Same Table

Dracula Jr. Still Wets the Coffin